Climbing the Mountain

Angela Aw

For book orders, email orders@traffordpublishing.com.sg

Most Trafford Singapore titles are also available at major online book retailers.

Printed in Singapore.

ISBN: 978-1-4907-0205-6 (sc)
ISBN: 978-1-4907-0206-3 (hc)
ISBN: 978-1-4907-0207-0 (e)

Trafford rev. 11/25/2013

 www.traffordpublishing.com.sg

Singapore
toll-free: 800 101 2656 (Singapore)
Fax: 800 101 2656 (Singapore)

CONTENTS

PREFACE

They had all the right ingredients for success and happiness. Mandy, the adoring wife. Barry, the pillar of strength. Then something happened. Mandy is plunged into darkness, caught in the depths of despair from a terminal disease. She turned to her pillar of strength. He handled the situation like he did in the war, with total and rigid control! He took care of everything like clockwork but due to his traumatic war experience, he could not give the one thing Mandy wanted, needed the most—his emotional support.

This book starts off with the experience of a soldier in a war-torn country. The trauma he could not overcome later dictated his married life. It also tells the intimate struggle of a young woman through cancer. It lets the reader glimpse at her life as an attractive and independent single woman to her married life which gradually robbed her of her true identity. Consequently, she realized that she had to pull through alone when the man she adored and looked up to showed his true self. She was left bewildered. Just when she hit rock bottom, it suddenly dawned on her that the only way left . . . . was the way up.

The road to recovery and reclaiming her identity was long and hard, but she pulled through with the patience and support of those who love her.

CHAPTER 1

Out of control

When Barry and his men reached Dong Van, they were greeted with hearty slaps on the back and a bottle of whiskey. Barry left them to their little celebration and followed the skinny lieutenant to the main tent to report.

Brigadier Chong looked up from behind his horn-rimmed spectacles as Barry flipped aside the tent cover and stepped in.

'Colonel Hawitt of the 1st Battalion of the Nangpa Regiment reporting, Sir!' Barry saluted his senior smartly.

'At ease, Colonel!' The older officer waved Barry to the vacant chair at his desk.

Barry recounted the journey and the lives lost in an 'as a matter of fact' fashion. Brigadier Chong stroked his well-trimmed moustache and trained his wise eyes on the young Colonel. He could see Barry's face was void of expression in what must have been an agitated situation. He decided to let the young man have a night of sound sleep before he told him his next orders. Barry was to see him again the next day.

Barry left the main tent and followed the skinny lieutenant to his own tent. He needed a bath. He was covered with grime and sweat from the journey. He wanted to wash himself free not only of the grime and sweat but also of the memory. He followed his ears to a river running by the camp. There was nobody there and Barry stripped down to his shorts and waded in.

He dipped his head under the clear running water, enjoying its coolness. The morning sun made the droplets of water glistened on his arms as he swept his wet hair back. The years of carrying sacks of wheat flour at the warehouse had paid off, giving him rippling biceps. He took the half cake of soap from the pocket of his shorts and started lathering himself.

He breathed in the scent of the soap as he generously soaped his muscular chest, his broad shoulders down to his washboard torso. He dipped himself into the running water again and swam for a few more minutes, enjoying the open sky framed by the branches and leaves of the jungle trees.

He almost felt reluctant to get out of the river. He towelled himself quickly with the coarse towel. He peeled off his wet shorts. Barry walked back to his tent in his army trousers, with the towel draped over his tanned naked shoulders.

When he slept that night, he dreamt again of the flare in the open field. As if somebody had pressed the 'slow' button on a video tape player, he saw vividly in slow motion how Private Minh and Danh got up first, followed by Duong and Hien. He saw how their bodies jerked from the impact of the bullets like somebody had whacked them from the back with a heavy bat. He saw their rifles dropping to the ground. He saw Private Danh half turned his body just before he too, fell to the ground, dead. It felt so unreal, like he was watching a tape instead of being there.

Three days later, they were on the move again. This time, they were passing through neutral territory. They travelled along a dirt road. It had not rained for a few days and the dirt covered their boots as they plodded along. The men were not too happy to leave the camp and their new found buddies behind. Barry was not happy either. He was tense and anxious. He did not sleep well in the camp. He held his rifle with his finger on the trigger, on the alert for the enemy. Lieutenant Huy and some of the men noticed. It gave them an uneasy feeling.

Every three or four kilometres, a small village would spring up. Thatched huts with half-naked children standing in front stared at them as they walked through. Children with uncombed hair and oversized clothes munching on stale buns, staring at them as if they were entertainment.

Suddenly there was a loud clap sound! Barry was seized with fear as he shouted, 'Take cover!'

The men immediately dispersed, the way ants do when they sensed danger while feasting on a scrap of food. They hid behind huts and carts, their rifles poised.

Somewhere a boy started laughing. He was dropping plastic bags of water from the roof of his hut! Apparently, he had seen the soldiers coming from a distance away and got ready for the mischievous act. The villagers were also laughing along with the boy.

Barry was filled with rage and stormed toward the boy. He climbed up to the roof and pulled the boy down. The teenage boy stopped laughing when he saw the look on Barry's face. He tried to run away but Barry grabbed his arm forcefully.

Once he dragged the boy down, he slapped him across his face. The shocked boy covered his slapped cheek and started crying but that did not stop Barry. He slapped him hard another time, his face full of fury. Before he could give the cowering boy another mighty slap, Lieutenant Huy grabbed his arm.

'Enough Colonel!'

Barry looked at him, his eyes wide with anger, his breathing ragged. Then he looked at his men who were all standing around him, a look of pity in their eyes. Barry shook free of the lieutenant's grasp, turned around and continued walking out of the village.

He knew he had overreacted. It was just a young boy playing tricks. He knew he had been on edge. It is just that he could not take losing any more men, men whom he fought with, men who looked up to him to keep them safe. He had lost his confidence to lead them. He had to get out of this. He would write a letter to the Major General, his uncle. He would request to be taken out of active duty, the sooner the better.

Angela Aw

True / False Statements. Circle the right answer.

1) Brigadier Chong was most likely reading when Barry entered his tent. T/F

2) Barry was older than Brigadier Chong. T/F

3) Barry and his men laughed at the teenage boy's tricks. T/F

4) Lientenant An stopped Barry from slapping the boy again. T/F

CHAPTER 2

Broken cries

B ombs were being dropped everywhere! People all around him were running for cover. There was confusion everywhere as the Japanese planes flew with ear-splitting sound overhead. The air was filled with smoke from the burning buildings. There were children standing and wailing, but their mother was nowhere to be seen. There were civilians covered in blood, half-dead, half-alive, groaning in pain. All around, there was the look of disbelief.

Barry Hawitt, Colonel of the 1st Battalion of the Nangpa Regiment was covered in blood too but it was not his blood. He was crouching down, holding Private Mang. The man was delirious with shock and pain. Part of his leg had been blown off by the bomb.

'Please don't let me die Colonel. I don't want to die. I want to go back to my family. I don't want to die. Help me Colonel, help me.'

Barry's lips pressed into a grim line at the plea.

Then he said with as much conviction as he could muster, 'You are going to live, man! You will live to go home, to see your family!"

The attack came all of a sudden, without warning. Normally the alarm would sound giving the soldiers and civilians time to run into the thick jungle, out of the buildings. But why, why didn't the alarm go off? All this could have been avoided.

Colonel Barry Hawitt, despite his rank was not much older than the private he was holding. He had been drafted into the armed forces at the age of 23. Eight months into his role, he was promoted to the rank of colonel. He accepted the post unwillingly. They needed men and Barry Hawitt looked like a man who could lead. He was quiet and he talked only when necessary. His manner was authoritative, having worked under his father who ran a well-oiled biscuits factory. His father had always told him to talk only when he had something important to say. He was a strict man, demanding all his 5 children to be prim and proper.

Just as suddenly as the attack started, it ended. Medical personnel were rushing to the wounded. Barry helped to carry Private Mang into the makeshift tent of a hospital. His severed leg was brought in too. The nurse saw Barry covered in blood and asked him if he was all right. Barry looked at the nurse and nodded his head, indicating he was all right. Then he turned on his heel and left the tent.

There were rubble and dead bodies left and right. Barry got to work and gave orders to his soldiers to get the wounded to the hospital first. He got some men to set up a temporary open-air kitchen. The women and children scavenged through the rubble for items that could be used, supplies, food, cooking utensils, anything that could be used. Barry got a few strong men and went off deeper into the jungle to look for more palm fronds to use as roofing. They had to make huts to sleep in at night. Nobody would dare to sleep out in the open where the planes might come back.

'Colonel Barry Hawitt?' She looked at him with her doe eyes.

'Yes, anything nurse?' Barry's voice was soft, he was tired.

'I don't know how to tell you this but . . . .' Her voice faltered and her eyes misted.

Barry looked at her, dread in his heart.

'He is gone. Private Mang is gone. We could not save him.' She began to sob. Barry walked away. He walked deeper into the jungle, away from the crowd. He walked and walked.

When he had gone a good distance, he sat down on a broken trunk. His shoulders were shaking as his tears flowed. He held his head as he cried, deep broken cries of a man who was unable to keep his promise.

A year later, the war ended. Barry stepped out of the plane, a hero. He was awarded medals for his courage and exemplary conduct in service. Barry accepted the bright and shiny medals but the war continued inside him.

Barry went back to work for his father at the biscuits factory. Soon he knew everything there was to running the business. His father handed it to him.

'Good morning, Mr. Hawitt!' Mandy Tang, his secretary greeted him as he walked into his office.

'Good morning, Mandy.' His greeting was cool as the morning air. Mandy had been working there for a month already. She had gotten used to her work and her office.

This was her first job. She had just finished school last year and went job hunting. Her uncle suggested she tried this company as it was established and could pay well.

'Why not try Hawitt's Biscuits?' Her uncle asked. 'They started before the war even began.'

'Who runs it now, Uncle?' Mandy's interest was heightened at the mention of this household name.

'I hear the eldest son, Barry Hawitt, expanded the company assets since he took over. Just 2 weeks ago, the supervisor who is a friend of mine told me his secretary resigned. She left to get married.'

'The position might already be filled.'

'You could still try, no harm in trying.' Her uncle cajoled.

Mandy called them up and found out the position was still vacant. An interview was arranged. When Barry first saw her, he had been reluctant to hire her because she was very young. As he interviewed her, he found out she was very independent and determined. She was also English-educated. That would be an advantage when it came to dealing with the foreign investors. Barry needed somebody with him on his business deals abroad, somebody who would learn the ropes quickly and be able to work on her own.

Questions

1) Who were attacking?

2) Who pleaded to be saved?

3) Why did the nurse ask if Barry was all right?

4) Why did Barry 'walk a good distance' after the nurse told him Private Mang could not be saved?

5) Who was Barry's new secretary?

6) What kind of business did Barry run?

CHAPTER 3

Back to the factory

'M andy?' Barry called her through his opened door. 'Would you come in here, please?'

Mandy hurriedly went in to his office. 'Yes, Mr Hawitt?' Mandy was a little nervous and in awe of Barry.

'I've a business trip on Friday to Hong Kong. I would like you to come along and do some paper work for me. It will only take 2 days. Can you come?'

Mandy's eyes widened and she quickly agreed. She had always loved to travel. She was an out-door person. During school time, she loved camping, picnicking and hiking with her friends. She was the one who organised the outing and called up her friends to join in. She planned parties and trips. She was very active and never lacked company.

After that first trip to Hong Kong, more trips followed. Mandy was getting used to handling the travel plans and hotel bookings. She even knew Barry's food preferences as they often had dinner together.

Barry's cool tone had also disappeared as he started appreciating Mandy's personality. Barry's eyes focused on Mandy as she was filling in some forms left by a client. She was so different, so young and vivacious. She was always the talkative one at dinner while Barry just smiled at her, amused.

Mandy looked up to Barry. He was so decisive and well-informed. He handled business efficiently and made sure things got done on time in the office. He was so fastidious.

Barry called Mandy at her house early one evening. He asked her if she had dinner already.

'It's too early for dinner. Is there something you want me to do?'

'Yes I would like to ask you out to dinner.'

Mandy was surprised but secretly pleased. She agreed and Barry said he would pick her up in half an hour's time.

Barry took Mandy to a quiet little place by the beach. They had a lovely dinner. Barry was charming and attentive. Mandy was flattered by this new side of him.

After dinner, Barry suggested a walk at the park nearby. The streets lamps lit the footways dimly and the air was cool.

They walked slowly, in silence. Suddenly Barry took Mandy's hand. She looked up at him. He pulled her close.

They went out almost every night after that. The rest of the staff started whispering among themselves that it was a foregone conclusion they were going to marry soon. They noticed their boss smiling and laughing more. There was an air of gaiety around him like happy sunshine where before there was a dark cloud over his head. The staff was no longer so terrified when they heard his car pull up at his parking lot.

'Barry, my sisters have just come back from England. I am having dinner with them at that new place in town. Come along with us?' Mandy coaxed, knowing Barry's dislike of a crowd.

'You know I don't like a big group of people! Go ahead and have fun with your sisters. I'll see you tomorrow.' Barry continued shifting through the documents, a frown on his forehead.

Mandy was taken aback by his sudden outburst. She retreated to her desk outside, troubled. Why did he say that? She was only going with her sisters; it was not like she was going out with another man. Why was he so angry? He did not have to put it that way even if he was angry. Maybe, he was just tired and stressed out with that fussy client who called earlier.

Barry's anger resurfaced when he saw Mandy's empty chair. She had left the office without him. She popped her head in to say goodbye but he just nodded his head without looking at her.

Mandy sounded so excited to have dinner with her sisters. No doubt they would be the centre of attraction when they walked in. Barry noticed men turning their heads to ogle at Mandy whenever they went out for dinner. They would stare at her show of fair legs beneath a short skirt. When Mandy laughed, even the waiter serving them seemed transfixed. Barry had told Mandy several times not to wear short skirts but she just answered that those were the only kind she had. Barry just did not like the kind of attention she was getting. Who knows what sort of men they may meet tonight?

It was just her youth, he reasoned. Women in his family don't dress like that. They were demure. Maybe she was too young for him, yet he felt drawn to her vivacity. He would influence her, he decided. After all, he could influence and command an army of men, what trouble is a young girl? He would tame her, make her less volatile. Then and only then could she be considered 'wife material'. He felt better now that he had a plan of action.

Barry was walking through the thick Nangpa jungle at night. They had to be careful; they were passing through enemy territory. Barry had received a radio call the night before. His orders were to move the men to regroup in Dong Van. He had no choice but to follow orders.

He had split his infantry into two groups. They had a better chance of survival this way. His lieutenant had radio called him to say they made it past the enemy territory and would be in Dong Van by early morning. He was relieved. That was also his cue to move the second half of the infantry. They smeared their faces with lines of ash and wore camouflage gear with leaves and twigs on their helmets and jackets.

Barry walked ahead of them. He bent his body low while carrying his rifle, his finger on the trigger, ever ready. His eyes were alert for any signs of the enemy. His men were spread out behind him. All they heard in the still of the night were the sounds of crickets chirping and owls hooting. His men were warned beforehand to maintain silence at all times. They were not even allowed to smoke and they used hand signals and imitate animal sounds to communicate. Not even the mosquitoes buzzing around their ears could distract them, they were all very tense. One wrong move and they could wind up dead.

After walking for some time, Barry could see a clearing up ahead. The scout he sent two days ago told him that beyond this clearing, there was a range of hills. Once they were past the hills, they would be safe.

They were almost past the clearing when a flare went up, lighting up the field, stripping the cover of darkness from them. Barry's heart started beating faster. Adrenaline surged through his veins as he yelled 'DOWN!' The men instinctively dropped to the ground. It rained gunshots. They were at a disadvantage being out in the open. His men realised this and a handful of them got up to run for cover back into the jungle.

'STAY DOWN!' Barry barked but it was no use. Those men panicked. They had not gotten a few steps when they were shot down.

Barry woke up in cold sweat, panting. He realised he was dreaming again. He looked at the clock and saw it was 4 o'clock in the morning. He dropped back on his pillow with his arms behind his head.

'If only those men had not panicked, if only he had trained them harder, if only . . . .'

After reading the reports filed, his seniors told him it was not his fault, that there are situations he could not possibly have complete control over. But to him, those men were his responsibility. Their lives were in his hands. In his mind, he had let them down; he had let the men's families down. He should have controlled them better, if only he had.

In Barry's mind, he must have complete control over any situation. He would leave nothing to chance. He reasoned that if he had complete control, then things would go his way. He felt comfortable and secure with this thought.

Questions

1) What did Mandy love to do?

2) Where did Barry take Mandy on their first business trip?

3) What is the staff's foregone conclusion?

4) What was Mandy so excited about?

5) Why did the soldiers smear their faces with ash?

6) What stripped the cover of darkness while the soldiers were passing through the clearing?

CHAPTER 4

Wholeheartedly

W hen Mandy got back to the office the next morning, Barry was already in. She was not very happy with Barry's outburst but kept quiet about it.

He was dressed in his usual favourite colour of brown, various shades of brown. Cream shirt and dark brown pants. A striped brown and white tie completed the outfit.

Mandy heart flipped when he smiled and greeted her with a warm 'Good morning!' She smiled her morning greeting in return, pleased and optimistic that that day would be a good day and everything was going to work out well.

'How was your dinner last night with your sisters?' He came over to her desk and perched on a corner, his arms folded, smiling.

'Great! The seafood at Arty's was scrumptious! We ordered baby squids fried with some kind of sweet, spicy sauce. It was served on a bed of crispy lettuce with tiny strips of green apple sprinkled on top! Mandy gushed on before Barry could comment. 'And the butter prawns were to die for! We could smell the prawns as the waiter was bringing it to our table! Butter and prawns go exquisitely well together.' Mandy licked her lips remembering the fragrance and taste of the juicy prawns.

'Was that all?' Barry took in her long wavy hair that cascaded over her shoulders. He noticed streaks of it gleamed a reddish brown in the sun. He had asked her if she dyed her hair but Mandy said she had never dyed her hair. It was natural as her mother too had hair of this colour.

'Oh no . . . . that was not all!' Mandy's eyes widened in protest as she cocked her head and clasped her hands in front of her chest.

'My eldest sister ordered the pineapple rice. It was served with raisins and meat floss in a carved out pineapple! My father said that we should get the recipe to try at home.' Mandy's eyebrows lifted in mock disbelief. Her enthusiasm over the food was so innocent and surprisingly refreshing.

'My sisters wanted ice cream for desert and we all ordered the same thing! I think it must be a family weakness.' Mandy pursed her lips together, nodding thoughtfully.

'Sounds like you had a great dinner!'

'Sure did! Delicious food and great company! But my sisters are leaving this afternoon.' Mandy sighed.

Barry stood up and swung Mandy's chair to face him. He leaned down with both his hands on the armrests and said, 'Tell you what, let's go back to Arty's for dinner next week. Would you like that?'

His face was so close to hers that Mandy could feel his breath on her. She stammered, 'Yyyesssss.' He gave her a quick kiss on her forehead and went into his office.

She gave herself a mental shake and tried to focus on her work but it was so difficult with Barry just a few feet away.

Barry proposed at dinner in Arty's the following week. Mandy breathlessly accepted and they were married one month later. After the wedding, Mandy moved into Barry's house where he stayed with his parents. He promised they would get their own house later.

Things happened very fast. Mandy got pregnant a couple of months later and gave birth to a healthy baby girl. Barry told Mandy to give up working in the office to stay and take care of the baby. Mandy readily agreed. She loved her husband very much and wanted to please him as much as she could. She dived into motherhood wholeheartedly. She breastfed her baby and slept with her in their bed.

It was not even a full year later that Mandy found out she was pregnant again. She gave birth to another baby girl, and another the following year. Life seemed perfect—three girls and a financially stable husband. Mandy willingly cancelled all her social life to take care of her family. Her children were very attached to her and demanded a great deal of her time. Mandy did not even have time for herself anymore. Due to the hot and humid weather, she walked around in shorts and old comfortable singlets like they were her daily uniform.

She did not have time to meet up with friends nor seek advice from her mother who lives in a village further north. Although she embraced her new role as a mother, there were times when she so wished her mother was around to help her raise the children and share her joy as the babies reached each milestone.

With the babies so close in age, it was like raising triplets! Mandy was relieved to have her younger sister, Long who came in to help during the school break. Two months later, Barry's sister, Hwa who had just completed her studies came in to take over Long's place as the school break was over. They were not much wiser in taking care of babies but Mandy was grateful for their help. They decided to hire a maid or two when Hwa had to leave.

'Ah . . . . , Hung is wet. She needs a diaper change.' Mandy laid her baby girl on the bed. Barry was combing his hair at the dressing table, getting ready to go to work.

'Why aren't there any fresh diapers here?' Mandy checked the drawer nearest to the bed. Hung was alert and busy wriggling her arms and legs in the air. Mandy had to open the other drawer just a step further away.

'Plop!' A dull thud sounded. Mandy immediately turned and saw her baby girl on the floor beside the bed! Her heart beat crazily as she moved with lightning speed to pick up her crying daughter to soothe her. Barry rushed over, full of concern. It was fortunate the bedstead was low and the floor was carpeted, cushioning her fall.

Baby Hung stopped crying in her mother's arm as she felt her kisses on her forehead and her voice telling her over and over again, 'You are all right. Mama is holding you now. Mama is holding you now.' Mandy would never forgive herself if something happened to any one of her babies.

Later on, when she related the incident to her aunt who was a more seasoned mother, Mandy's knees were still weak from fright. Her aunt laughed at her, telling her it was all right. There was nothing to be so terrified of. The babies became her life, the house became her world.

Her topics for conversation centred on the babies and the marketing. She neither watched television nor listened to the radio. Barry humoured her at first by responding and listening to what she had to say about the babies. As time went by and the babies grew, he became more and more involved in the speech and character development of Hung, Kim and Lan.

Barry turned out to be every child's dream father. Mandy was gratified to see such a reaction from Barry.

She was still breastfeeding the babies. It was at this time Mandy started having a sore nipple. She did not think too much of it as she had put some cream on it. To her, the babies came first before all else, even her own needs.

It felt like she woke up at the crack of dawn and went at breakneck speed the rest of the day. Most of the time, it felt like motherhood was a 24-hour shift 7 days a week.

One night, her baby girl was crying in her cot. Mandy was deep in sleep but she pulled herself up by sheer determination and went to prepare a bottle of milk as fast as her still groggy mind would allow. She always handled the babies alone at night unless all the babies cry simultaneously. As was her habit, she would quickly gulp down a mouthful of water before making the milk. Her room was dimly lit by the night light. She had always left her tumbler of plain water beside the tin of milk powder. She opened her mouth to drink the water, no quenching water came and her nose told her the water smelled strange. Why did the water smell of milk?

She squinted at the bottle and realised it was the tin of milk she was holding instead!

'Thank goodness I did not pour the whole tin of milk powder on my face!' Mandy laughed in her heart, amazed that such a thing could happen. She resolved to put her water tumbler in a different position.

Sometimes, she wondered if mothers who worked in the office had a better deal. At least they had other topics to talk about; they had other people to talk to. But then she knew she could never leave her babies while they were still so young.

She knew the babies needed her and she enjoyed taking care of them. Yet somehow, she still felt stressed. She longed for the days when Barry and her would be together watching a movie or taking an after-dinner walk, enjoying the cool night air and the star-lit sky.

Although she felt something was lacking, she told herself that this was just a phase of her life and there would be good times again with Barry. The babies' crying pulled her thoughts back to the present as she hurriedly went to see her darlings.

Fill in the blanks.

1) Mandy's family has a weakness for eating

   _____.

2) Barry proposed at _____.

3) Barry and Mandy had _____ babies.

4) Baby _____ fell down the bed.

5) Barry only gets up to feed a baby if both _____
   simultaneously.

6) Mandy longed for time alone with _____.

CHAPTER 5

A persistent sore

Mandy was now twenty-six years old and had three lovely children. She was content living the life of a housewife, doing daily cooking and cleaning for the family.

After months and many trips to and fro the doctor, finally the result of the biopsy came. The news was devastating. She had cancer.

"Why is this happening to me?" she thought.

"Am I going to die?" She was going through the initial stages of shock and denial.

Although the doctor said she would send the biopsy specimen for a second testing at a private laboratory just to confirm the result of the first testing, Mandy felt numb.

She was suddenly gripped by fear. She thought of her young innocent children who always trusted her, who look to her for everything. How are they going to manage without her? Are they going to grow up motherless? Who will guide them in their teenage years?

She felt angry and wrongfully robbed of the joy of raising her children, of watching them grow, of passing on her values to them.

"Is this how it is going to be? Is this how my life is going to end?" She cried out bitterly, tears streaming down her cheeks.

It started out as a sore nipple. She thought it was caused by the constant suckling by Lan, the youngest daughter who refused to give up her favourite source of milk supply.

Whenever that nipple got sore, she would let Lan suckle from her other breast, giving the injured breast time to heal. After some weeks, it did heal and she continued breast-feeding from both sides. But then it would get sore again. So this went on, the sore and the healing, for months and months.

It was a minor nuisance having to apply medication and taking longer than usual in the bathroom. She told her husband, Barry but she didn't think more of it as she was extremely busy taking care of her children who were very demanding.

Her husband also didn't think much of it either as he had just bought a house and was busy renovating it, trying to get it ready of the coming festive season. Whenever he was not at the new house to supervise the renovation work, he would be at home pouring over the plans of the new house.

It wasn't as if she did not seek any medical advice. When it was time to bring the children for their scheduled check-up at the polyclinic, she did take the opportunity to ask the nurse there. The nurse gave her a tube of cream, saying it was good for healing sores caused by breastfeeding.

She thought it was a persistent sore and that perhaps she should see a doctor but never in her wildest dream did she think it was cancer. Daily, she saw to it that the children were bathed and fed properly. She made sure they took their naps and vitamins. She kept them occupied with books for children, taught them how to hold a pencil, sang songs to them and brought them out for walks around the house.

Although she had two live-in maids to help her with her children, Mandy felt frazzled, having to plan the menu, for her family and her in-laws. She did the marketing, often waking up early in the morning to get to the fish market in the hope that she would be able to buy some good quality fresh fish. Fellow marketers would comment on the amount of vegetables she bought, often asking her if she was buying vegetables to last for a whole week when in fact it was only for three days. Others would comment that she ought to use a trolley instead of a basket to carry the heavy amount.

She was so on edge in taking care of the children that she neglected herself. Her T-shirts had holes in them because they were so well-worn. She cut her waist—length hair to a boyish look to cut short her time in the bathroom. Her skin-care routine was almost nonexistent. She was always in a hurry as there was much to be done each day.

She was wise in planning the maids' daily duties and checked that they did a good job. The maids felt the pressure of their work, constantly watching over the kids for fear they would fall or injure themselves.

Mandy realised that good help was hard to find. One of the maids who was fresh from a nearby village was so insolent; she couldn't get along with anybody. Mandy had a good mind to fire her since she became a constant thorn in one's flesh but Barry constantly reminded her that help of any kind is near to impossible to find.

Not surprisingly, when the other maid moved on to a new venture after a year, Mandy knew she really had to square her shoulders to tolerate the insolent maid.

There was a time the remaining maid was stressed and decided to let it show. She was cooking at the stove and when she saw Mandy coming into the kitchen, she threw a metal spoon halfway across the room into the kitchen sink. "C L A N G!"

Mandy was carrying one of the babies at that time. Her blood temperature soared upon the maid's provoking gesture. Mandy reminded herself her baby girl was in her arms.

She kept telling herself, "I'm carrying the baby," over and over again. Luckily, the baby in her arms prevented her from resorting to violence. She left the kitchen pretending she didn't witness anything out of the ordinary.

Perhaps it was stress like this that led to the cancer, perhaps it was something else. Whatever it was, she knew she had to tolerate it for the sake of her children as her husband's advice kept reverberating in her head.

"Just another two years," she kept telling herself. "Then it would be good riddance!" She consoled herself with the thought that she would celebrate the maid's expiry of contract with a party or a dinner out with friends. She started to smile as she thought of her friends and the good time they were going to have.

Questions:

1) What was Mandy's illness?

2) How old was Mandy when she gave birth?

3) How did Mandy feel upon discovering her illness?

4) How did Mandy keep her children occupied?

5) What kind of problem did Mandy have with one of her maids?

6) What did the insolent maid do to make Mandy angry in the kitchen?

CHAPTER 6

Confused

M andy was scared. She needed somebody to talk to. She needed more information. She could not keep this inside her. Her doctor kept telling her that her best option was an operation.

Mandy turned to her close friend and tearfully told her tale. Her friend then told her that it would be a good idea to get more information from another woman who had gone through the same situation. Mandy was sceptical because she was living in a small town.

Her doctor said they would also remove her lymph nodes. These are situated at the armpit and when they are removed, she would have to take extra care of the affected arm.

'The lymph nodes are a collecting point, a first line of defence for the body if there are invaders, in this case, cancer. If it is found that cancer has spread to these lymph nodes or if there is a risk, they would have to be removed to prevent further infection or metastasis as is the medical term.' Doctor Kong was talking to Mandy and Barry in his clinic. Mandy sat there listening but it was as if the doctor was talking about someone else, not her.

He continued, 'So if the first line of defence is removed, then any wound like a cut from a dirty knife or even a mosquito bite would best be avoided as it would take longer to heal or something worse.'

Mandy went to the internet to find out if removal of the lymph nodes was necessary. The other woman expressed surprise. That was when Mandy started to have doubts about the operation.

She called up her surgeon who was kind enough to give her house phone number and asked Mandy to call her later that night. Mandy was very tense as she was quite intimidated by the lady surgeon who seemed to put everybody around her quite ill at ease. She was briefed by her husband on what to ask and that made her even more nervous.

As she called up the surgeon, they talked and the lady surgeon told her how important it was to have the operation done soon. They then discussed a possible date and tentatively agreed so the surgeon could book the operation theatre.

Barry disagreed, saying, 'That is not a good date. It is too close to the public holidays, the hospital would be handled by a skeleton crew.'

Mandy's heart sank thinking that she had to call the surgeon again to change the date after what seemed like such a tedious task of setting the date in the first place.

So Mandy called up again and surprisingly, the surgeon was agreeable. She just had to check if the operation theatre was free for that date and she would call back to confirm with Mandy.

As the operation date drew closer, Mandy felt more and more nervous. Two days before departing on the seven-hour drive to the city where the operation was to be performed, Mandy had cold feet. Barry was just leaving for work in a hurry trying the get the necessary papers ready for the trip when Mandy plucked up the courage and told him, "No, I don't want to go for the operation. I need some time I want to go for a second opinion at that private hospital."

Barry, somewhat exasperated said, "Are you sure? You know time is of the essence here."

"I am sure."

"All right . . . . I respect your decision."

Barry's eyes brightened at the more logical choice. He left for work. For Mandy, it was a relief. She did not want to have any doubts about the operation or have any regrets after it.

So through another friend who was a doctor, Mandy made an appointment to see a surgeon in a private hospital.

Mandy went with her husband and her children to see the surgeon. Dr Lim seemed to be a man of experience. He was certainly a very patient man; he answered Mandy's entire list of questions without her even asking him! That impressed Mandy and won her trust. He also examined Mandy.

"Do you know you have a lump here?"

"Yes."

Mandy reached to feel the lump and to her surprise, it was bigger than the last time she felt it. And the last time she felt could not be more than three or four weeks ago!

"It seems bigger than the last time I felt it," confessed Mandy.

After the examination, Dr. Lim told her that having a lump with a sore nipple is a very serious matter, one that needed urgent attention. He was puzzled as to why it took so long to have the operation done since the time the condition was first discovered.

Mandy explained that a year went by before she received any medical attention for her breast since she was housebound taking care of her children. No doubt she had maids who helped her but the actual care of the children fell on her shoulders. But if she had any suspicion that it was cancer, she would have seen a doctor. Furthermore, her sore came and went, just like a rash.

And when she finally did see a doctor, even the doctor could not confirm it was cancer until the biopsy. Even the biopsy was delayed as Mandy wanted to try the cream to see if the sore would heal.

So now that the biopsy was done, double checked and the second opinion sought, Mandy knew what she had to do.

Even though the surgeon charged Mandy a hundred dollars for an hour's consultation, she felt it was worth it having all her questions answered. Now she could go ahead with a peace of mind.

Still, she dreaded the days ahead.

Questions:

1) When did Mandy have doubts about the operation?

2) What happens when lymph nodes are removed?

3) Who thought the operation date was not suitable?

4) When did Mandy get cold feet?

5) How did the second surgeon impress Mandy?

6) Why was Mandy surprise at the examination?

CHAPTER 7

The inevitable

S o now that her condition was confirmed and she had her second opinion, there was nothing to keep her from the operation. Mandy rang up her lady surgeon to fix the operation date.

Mandy and Barry were worried about the children since she had never been apart from them, not even for a few hours. Now she would be hospitalized for possibly a few days, maybe even a week!

"Have you written the list on what to bring for the trip?" asked Barry.

"Yes, I have."

"Don't forget to tell the maid what to pack too. She can pack the kitchen stuff and you do the rest."

Mandy was worried enough about the impending operation. Having to do the packing irked her. She was even more concerned that her husband would not be able to cope with the children since he was not used to handling them alone.

When Hung, Kim and Lan were younger, Mandy and Barry used to take the children for evening car rides. He would come home and changed out of his work clothes and hurried downstairs to the waiting family. It was the family's

---

only outing. Mandy and her children looked forward to the car ride each day. Then one day, Barry decided to take a different route home . . . . all of a sudden, Lan started to cry, terrified. She was crying and looking out of the window.

The new parents were distressed but could not figure out why Lan was crying. No matter what both the father and mother said, the child continued to cry.

Later on, they found out that it was because of a crane that was shifting things at a construction site. It was huge, noisy; puffing out smoke and that caused the baby to cry.

During the renovation of their new house, he had to make several trips to Kimanli just a couple of hours away by car. Each time he went, Mandy wished that he would bring the children and her along. How many times she cajoled and pleaded with him but he seemed unmoved until one day . . . . he agreed!

So it was a day trip, five hours by car, round the town to shop for furniture and then lunch, a little shopping and then another five-hour-ride back. Mandy was ecstatic! It had been years since she had an outing like that.

During the car ride, Mandy talked almost non-stop to her toddlers, calming them and occupying their thoughts with the world passing outside the car windows. It was exhilarating!

She had a great time seeing the world through the eyes of her children. All too soon, it was time for the journey home. The toddlers were tired and started getting cranky. They missed their usual afternoon nap.

Over the phone, Barry told his sister, "Glad that we did not stay overnight with the kids. They were already longing for home."

Mandy interrupted, "I think they were just tired from the trip and they had not taken their afternoon nap. I am confident that they would not be whining if we stayed overnight in a hotel."

After a few more day trips, Barry decided to take a chance to stay overnight in a hotel in the nearby town. He called another two of his aunties along too, for extra help.

Mandy and the children were delighted to stay a night in another place other than their own home. This soon became a trend in their trips out of town.

It was a new experience, handling the children away from home. The real challenge was about to come. Mandy would soon undergo the operation and leave the children under the care of Barry and the maid, Nancy.

Mandy had to go in a day earlier to prepare and fast for the operation. The junior doctors came and tried to draw some blood from her arm for preliminary testing. They said it was normal procedure in case the patient undergoing operation would suddenly need extra blood.

"Just relax; this will only take a minute," said Doctor Mary.

Mandy could feel the prick of the needle as it went in.

"Something is wrong," thought Mandy. "Why is it taking so long?"

It felt like the doctor inserted the needle into her arm and TWISTED it slowly. It was painful, Mandy winced.

"Did you get any blood?" asked Mandy, not daring to look.

The doctor did not answer immediately but went to the other side of the bed.

'I'm sorry that was not successful. I have to try on this arm.' Mandy braced herself for the next assault.

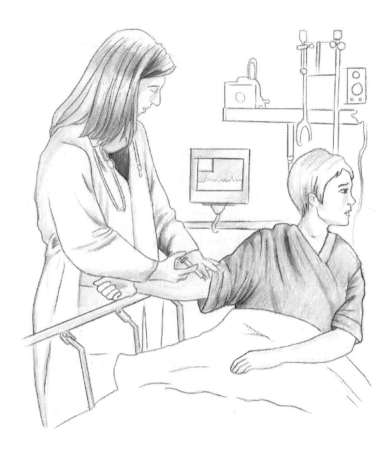

She heaved a sigh of relief when she saw the syringe full of dark thick blood.

The next morning, Mandy waited and waited, tense. She had gotten up very early before dawn to bathe and had changed into the white hospital gown. Finally at ten, the nurse came and told Mandy to be ready. They put the cap on her and pushed her to the operation theatre.

Mandy was nervous and felt completely helpless on the trolley, like a lamb being led to the slaughter. Thankfully, the anaesthetic put her out along with any feelings of anxiety.

"We can only tell you how far your cancer has progressed after the operation, after the specimen has been sent for testing." These words kept repeating themselves in Mandy's mind as she lay there waiting and waiting.

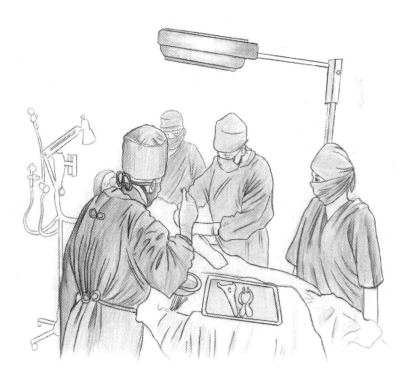

True or False statements. Circle the correct answer.

1) Mandy was worried about the children because she had never been away from them. T/F

2) Her 1st born started crying whenever they took an unfamiliar route home. T/F

3) Mandy was not excited on her first trip out of town. T/F

4) Barry told her that the children were longing for home on the drive home. T/F

5) The doctor was unsuccessful in drawing blood from Mandy the first time. T/F.

6) Mandy felt helpless as they wheeled her in for her operation. T/F.

CHAPTER 8

Hope

It took five hours for the operation for it was a major operation. They removed some of her lymph nodes. Mandy woke up in the ward, feeling weak. She was incredibly thirsty but could only take sips of water.

'Don't drink too much. You will vomit,' warned the nurse.

Barry was there and he had employed a local maid to help. She would stay the night at Mandy's side. When Mandy woke up, it was evening. She had slept most of the day.

That night was the worst night for her. The nurses said it was the after effects of the anaesthetic. It made her very uneasy. She asked to be helped to the toilet to empty her bladder but they made her use a bedpan. Mandy protested against the cold bedpan and just could not empty her bladder.

After several minutes of futile attempts and a still dry bedpan, her maid gave in and agreed to help Mandy to the toilet. She pressed the buzzer to call a nurse in to help support Mandy to the toilet.

It seemed to hurt every muscle in her body just to sit up but Mandy was determined to get to the toilet. She just felt soooo uneasy! It was quite troublesome as there were two tubes attached to her operation site.

It was also a very humbling experience sitting on the toilet with a total stranger just in front. She went back to her bed after she finished her business.

One or two minutes after the nurse and her maid got her into bed, she asked to go again! She said that she just felt so uncomfortable. So this happened another two more times, going to and fro the toilet. Mandy was just as exasperated, not wanting to cause anybody trouble but unable to help herself.

After the toilet trips, she asked to be helped to sit on the chair next to her bed, she just could not sleep. "Please God . . . . don't let this uneasiness carry on to the next night!" begged Mandy in her heart.

Her maid protested strongly saying "But Madam! You have just come out of your operation! Please don't move around so much, you might start to bleed!"

"Please . . . . I can't sleep . . . I feel soooo uneasy. Just help me to the chair and I will be all right."

With a sigh, the maid slipped her strong arm under Mandy's back while she grabbed the maid's other arm for support and sat upright. She liked the way the maid held her close. It made her feel secure, that there was no chance of her falling back on the bed or the maid losing her grip, both of which would cause Mandy incredible pain.

Barry and children came almost every day to see her. Her children always came close to her, they needed to touch and smell their mother. They had never been separated from her, not even for a few hours.

For Mandy, it was such a delight to see her children, to hold them close, to kiss and smell them. It brightened up her day to see the happy smiles on their cute faces and to hear them say "I love you mummy!"

After a week, it was time for Mandy to be discharged. It was such a wonderful surprise when one of her old friends came to the hospital to see her! If there is one thing you should know about staying in a hospital, it is that it is very depressing. Your world is suddenly downsized to one room! Sure, you can try to occupy your time with books and magazines but they can only take up so much of your time.

Mandy read somewhere that cancer is a disease that not only attacks the body, but the mind and the spirit as well. Your body already has cancer, your mind is thinking how long you are going to live and your spirit is low because everything you do does not seem to matter since you are going to die anyway. People will say that everybody is going to die one day but who really thinks about it? But for a person with cancer, the threat is very real and it is a threat that is ALWAYS there! It colours everything that person does.

Mandy started to question her own life. Has she been living a meaningful life? Is she happy? Or has she been trying to fit into the mould created for another person?

A few days after she was discharged, she was told to go back to the hospital to have the stitches removed. While waiting, she asked her lady doctor what stage of cancer she was in.

'Your lymph nodes are clear . . . . have you gone for a liver ultrasound?'

Mandy was puzzled, if she had not asked the doctor that question; would the liver ultrasound be suggested?

A liver ultrasound is a procedure that checks the liver for anything that is not normal, like cancer cells.

The lady who did the ultrasound on Mandy also checked all her abdominal organs and told her they were clear! This was good news; it meant that the cancer did not spread. It did not spread to her lymph nodes or her other organs. She had a chance to live!

On the way back, in the car alone with her husband, Mandy said, "I am incredibly lucky! Just think, I have this condition for ONE WHOLE YEAR!" Barry concurred.

When her doctor told her she has cancer, Mandy thought she was going to die for sure, her days were numbered. It was only much later, during a meeting with Doctor Patsy, an oncologist, that Mandy asked and found out she was in stage one. Doctor Patsy was a well-known cancer specialist.

In cancer, they count from stage 0 to stage 5. Stage 0 is without lump. The stage goes up depending on the size of the lump or tumour. Mandy could have been in stage 0 and need not have her lymph nodes removed if she had gone for the operation earlier, before the lump appeared.

Again Mandy thought back to the time she first discovered it. Her nipple DID heal. She TOLD Barry when it became sore again but as her mind was totally pre-occupied with her kids and household, her health slipped her mind.

Fill in the blanks:

1) The maid who helped Mandy during her hospital stay was a _____.

2) The night _____ the operation was the worse for Mandy.

3) The children _____ to touch and smell their mother whenever they came to visit her.

4) Cancer is an attack on the body, mind and _____.

5) A liver ultrasound is a procedure that checks the _____.

6) A cancer specialist is called an _____.

CHAPTER 9

The journey begins

After the meeting with the oncologist, Mandy learned that she had to undergo chemotherapy and radiotherapy. This is a cancer treatment where they inject toxic drugs into your body to kill the cancer cells.

Mandy heard that chemotherapy is a very difficult process; many suffer from the side effects.

Doctor Soon who was the local town doctor said to Mandy, 'Stick with the treatment, no matter how difficult. I know of a lady who gave up the treatment secretly. She told everybody she was still undergoing chemotherapy but she was not. She could not take the side effects. She died in the end.'

Aunt Prilla had a friend who underwent chemotherapy. Aunt Prilla sympathised with Mandy.

She told Mandy, 'The most obvious side effect of chemo is the loss or thinning of hair. You lose hair all over your body. People may tell you that you will not lose your hair, maybe not all but you will lose some.'

For Mandy, the first chemo went reasonably well. It took only an hour for the process to be completed but she was there at the hospital the whole morning just waiting.

She was given some pills to relieve the nausea and vitamins because the drugs kill not only the cancer cells but the good healthy ones as well.

"Ling and his wife are downstairs waiting to see you." said Barry.

Mandy just got back from her first chemo and was lying on the bed, "Errr . . . . , I don't think I can get up to see them."

Mandy lay down for as long as she could that afternoon, even until after the Lings left. Then she had to go to the toilet. The minute she reached the toilet, she started vomiting her lunch into the toilet bowl.

What was so torturing was the fact that she had to swallow handfuls of pills to stop vomiting but even the mere act of drinking water caused her to vomit. Mandy brought a small bucket with her everywhere she went, just in case she had to vomit. But swallow the pills she did!

She was sick for almost a week. She was lying down most of the time, her stomach felt like it was full of gas, and she did not have any appetite to eat or drink but forced herself to. She did not have any mood to do anything, not even to read a book or to watch television.

Barry asked her when they could head back home. Sensing her husband's unease, she agreed to go home after staying in Keena for almost two weeks.

"Can you board the plane with the help of the airport staff while we drive back?" Barry asked.

"Under normal circumstance, I can but I feel so unfocused now!"

"Then you better call your sister to come and accompany you back to Sooba."

"Yes, that would be good."

Mandy was glad her sister agreed to come just to accompany her from Keena airport to Sooba. Her vision was affected, blurred and she could not even think straight. She could not concentrate properly when people were talking, she felt like a zombie.

It was the night before they were to leave for home that Mandy started experiencing back pain. She slept poorly because of the intense pain. She forced herself to get up and help get the kids ready for the journey. She thought it was the side-effects of the chemo that was causing her the pain.

Mandy arrived in Sooba earlier than her family who got there by car. They spent a night in her parents' place. That night her eldest daughter started coughing very badly. Mandy's back continued to cause her intense pain, the pain being especially bad at night. Mandy hoped that Barry would get up to use the inhaler on their daughter but he did not. He was exhausted from driving all the way from Keena to Sooba, six hours in all. Mandy got up slowly, wincing from the effort, got the inhaler and used it on her daughter.

The next morning, Mandy was still in great pain. She got up from her bed and went straight to the sofa. She did not go to brush her teeth or wash her face. Her mother massaged her back providing temporary relief.

'Are you sure you can make the journey back?' Mandy's mother asked with a frown on her face.

'I have to, Ma. My kids are there.'

'Do you want me to go with you?'

'Thanks Ma, that would be great.' Mandy managed a smile. She left for Mutalin by plane accompanied by her mother that afternoon.

She had three weeks to rest before her next chemo. Her back pain did not subside till after a week. She took some painkillers and went to bed. She would sleep soundly for an hour or two and then the pain would come again, jolting her awake. If you believe in superstitions, it was as if somebody had made a miniature doll of her and was hammering on her back.

Hammer, stop for a few seconds, hammer, stop, on and on it went till morning.

Mandy's mother had given her a mini massager and she went to the living room just outside her bedroom to use it. It was a little noisy and she did not want to wake up her sleeping family. She lay there, night after night, in pain, in tears.

A few days before she was scheduled to go for her second chemo, she had to report to the head doctor in her town. There, she asked if there was any medication for her pain since ordinary painkillers did not work. The doctor prescribed a sedative to ease the pain and help her sleep at night.

The circumstances of her second chemo were so unexpected it brought Mandy's spirit down to the very bottom. She thought that it would be just a morning of waiting and then the injection of the chemo drugs would begin. But it was not so. She went to the hospital at 7am and waited till 4pm because the small rural hospital had only one doctor on duty! Mandy was so depressed staying in the ward full of patients. She was given a bed and when she felt tired from sitting on the plastic chair, she lay down on the bed.

The nurse came to put the needle into her vein for the chemo drugs. Mandy was already scared and nervous. When the nurse failed, Mandy could not hide her tears. She hated crying in front of strangers, in public and tried to stop her tears. Thank God, the nurse got it on the second try.

Mandy lay on her hospital bed feeling so depressed. Being in there reminded her that her cancer was so real, so real and she was being treated for it, not knowing if she would survive. She was crying on and off the whole day. When they finished injecting all the drugs into her and she could go home, Mandy was drained physically and emotionally.

She got home, went into the bathroom and vomited many times. She looked into the mirror and thought, "What a sight you are! Your face is swollen and the pain is so obvious on your face!" Even when she thought there was nothing left to vomit, she still vomited. It was such an uncomfortable feeling. She put a small bucket close to her bed for fear that she might not reach the toilet in time.

When her head hit the pillow, she slept. She was so thankful her day of ordeals was over and she could finally rest.

So that was her second chemo. In another three weeks and she would be having her third chemo.

"Please God; let me be able to handle the next chemo better," Mandy prayed.

Questions

1) What kind of treatment did Mandy have to undergo after her meeting with the oncologist?

2) What did Mandy carry around with her everywhere she went for almost a week after chemotherapy?

3) Who accompanied Mandy by plane from Keena to Sooba?

4) How many weeks did Mandy have to rest before the next chemotherapy?

5) How did Mandy feel going for the treatment in the hospital?

6) How did Mandy look like after her treatment?

CHAPTER 10

Turbulent seas

T he saying that cancer is an attack not only on the body, but also on the mind and the spirit and that proved to be especially true during Mandy's third chemo treatment.

As usual, she had to go to the polyclinic lab to have her blood tested. The usual lab technician was out for breakfast so Mandy agreed to let this new man try after finding out if he was experienced.

She was nervous and tried not to let it show for fear this would make the finding of the vein unsuccessful. She looked away when he injected the syringe.

"Unsuccessful", he said. "Let's try another different spot."

After he pulled out the syringe the second time, still empty, he said apologetically, "I'm sorry I cannot do it. Can you go down to one of the nurses downstairs? I think they would be able to do it better."

Mandy laughed uneasily, "Ya, I don't think I want to let you try again either."

Instead of going to the nurses downstairs, Barry went to the hospital where they were successful the last few times. Perhaps she should not have mentioned the man at the polyclinic failed because this only made the lab technicians in the hospital even more jumpy.

John pushed Mary to have a go first but Mary pushed him back instead. It seemed like they were having a tug of war! Finally John agreed to try on Mandy first. Mandy liked John and was confident he could do it.

When he failed, Mandy was near panic, "Oh no, this is the third unsuccessful try! Now Mary is my LAST HOPE! What will they do if she fails???"

When Mary inserted the syringe, Mandy prayed,

"Please . . . . let her find my vein . . . . please . . . ."

Mary silently shook her head as she pulled out the yet empty syringe. This time, Mandy could not hold it together anymore. Her tears flowed freely down her cheeks and though she tried to think of all the funny email jokes her friends sent her, they provided little comfort at a time when fear reigned supreme.

No matter how hard she tried to stem the flow of tears, she could not. She was also aware of how uncomfortable this made the staff. She was also keenly aware of Barry standing a distance away, arms folded, silent.

She saw the backdoor and headed straight for it. She had only three pieces of tissue paper in her tote bag. She wished she had brought along a big towel handkerchief instead. She was so unprepared for today! Who would have thought that they needed to jab her four times already and still could not get any blood. Instead all they got were rivers of tears!

Outside the backdoor there was no cover still, just a few steps of a stairwell and no wall or anything to hide behind. All Mandy could do was just to cover her face with the last remaining soaking wet tissue and sob and sob. Her hand phone rang but she ignored it, lost in her fear.

After a few minutes, the head nurse came, saw Mandy still crying on the stairs, stroked her back and went inside to give her a few more minutes to calm down.

When Mandy went in, she saw that Barry was just about to come out and get her. She sat down in the same chair waiting for the head nurse.

The nurse rubbed some anaesthetic cream on a prominent vein on her forefinger. After a few minutes, she got her syringe of blood! Phew! What a relief!

Mandy had calmed down and was getting up to leave when the head nurse hugged her, stroked her back and said soothing words to her. This comforted her a great deal and her tears started flowing again.

She cried all the way back home. Once Barry dropped her off outside the front gate, she went upstairs to her bedroom, locked the door, sat on the floor and cried the whole morning.

She decided that she was going to take up her friend's offer to accompany her to the next chemo. She so badly needed someone who could talk and distract her, take her mind off the fear and nervousness every time a syringe is jabbed into her.

She didn't know if this was going to embarrass Barry but she went ahead with it anyway.

Once they reached the hospital compound, Barry parked his car. Mandy could see her friend waiting at the entrance.

She casually said, 'Oh! There's Lenny. She is coming to the chemo with me.'

Barry looked surprised but did not say anything. She needed reinforcement and she was going to get it.

When the nurse was getting ready to insert the needle, Mandy's facial expression changed. Her eyes suddenly turned red and filled. Luckily, her friend Lenny was sensitive enough to notice, acknowledged it and made it into a joke. Lenny kept Mandy talking about other topics as the nurse did her job.

Amazingly not a drop of tear fell that day. Mandy was so thankful she didn't have that fear or had to go through embarrassing bouts of tears in front of strangers. She knew then that her friend Lenny was the key to overcoming that fear.

So she went through the remaining three chemo treatments fearlessly. Each and every time, her friends Lenny and Sandra would come to accompany her during the drawing of blood and when they inserted the needle into her arm. They would bring treats and their chatter somehow filled Mandy up and chased away all the misery that accompanies hospital stays.

Each chemo treatment was different for Mandy. Sometimes the side effects were mild and she could start eating and drinking the very next day and at other times, she would continually feel bloated and nauseous.

But always, Mandy made it a point not to stay depressed and idle in the house. She went out for car rides on her own and strolled at the local market even though the doctor warned her not to go to crowded places because of her lowered immunity system. She had to as she could not stay at home without any distraction. She tried to keep as healthy as she could by exercising on the treadmill or going for morning walks. She forced herself to eat and drink even when she had absolutely no appetite or thirst.

Mandy started getting in touch with her long-lost buddies and family through emails and the phone. What could she do? She could not do much or any household chores and the only way to distract her mind was through her writing. Mandy had a passion for writing; it was her secret garden, one which she could escape to for hours, free from the morbid thoughts of her condition. Her network of friends and family became her support.

Finally the day came for her last chemo. It did not seem possible that this day would arrive but it did. Mandy went to the hospital as usual. She waited and waited. The doctor came and told her that they misplaced her drugs in another town 2 hours away! But they had already sent somebody there to get it.

They finally got her drugs at 4pm. Mandy had been waiting with the needle in her arm since 9am. She did not entertain any thoughts that they may not get the drugs to her in time and she might have to come in again the next day. No matter what, that was her last chemo and nothing could dampen her spirit. She even got a bouquet of flowers that day! They finally finished with her at 5minutes to midnight! Mandy was so happy she was smiling on her way home.

She was singing in her heart, "Finally, the worst is over. I made it, I made it!"

True / False statements. Circle the right answer.

1) They jabbed Mandy 6 times just before her 3rd chemo. T/F

2) Barry was not there at her 3rd drawing of blood. T/F

3) Mandy cried at the stairwell. T/F

4) Lenny did not come to distract Mandy. T/F

5) Mandy found things to do to keep from being depressed. T/F

6) Mandy's last chemo finished at 5 minutes to midnight. T/F

CHAPTER 11

Time for changes

M andy had been crying all morning. She wanted to go to her parents' house which was in Sooba. She was still weak and in pain. She had not been to her parents' house in years.

He came up to the bedroom. Mandy, half hyperventilating said,

"Barry, I want to take a break." Silence.

Mandy swallowed and pushed on, "Barry, I NEED to take a break."

"What did you say? I didn't hear you."

Mandy said in a louder, stronger voice, "I NEED to take a break."

"The doctor said that you will have a break, one month's break before your radiotherapy."

"I don't mean that kind of break."

"Aren't you taking a break everyday?"

Mandy tensed up again and although her heart was beating furiously, she pushed on, "I want to follow my mother home to her place to take a break. I told you this many months ago."

Silence again, as usual. Barry went to bed, puzzled. Mandy went on with the rest of the day, her heart glad she said what she wanted to say, but at the same time, there was an uneasy feeling in her heart.

"Why? Why can't I take a break? Why is it so difficult for me to go home, to rest and recuperate? I have not been home in 7 years! I miss home! I miss the peace and tranquillity, the sound of rivers flowing, birds chirping, the smell of the roses in my mother's garden!"

Mandy went home with her mother a few days later with a heavy heart. She almost changed her mind about going but decided it was in her best interest to go. She needed this break so badly.

She was sick when she arrived in Sooba. All she could do was to dump her bag on the floor and lay down on the sofa, in tears. She lay there for hours until Endrica came.

She cried everyday for a whole week. Only later, when her friends started coming to see her did she brighten up. She stayed in Sooba for a month before proceeding to Keena for her radiotherapy.

Her one-month-stay in Sooba did wonders for her mental well-being. It is no wonder that cancer patients are encouraged to go on a holiday. A change of scene took all of Mandy's depression away.

She had not intended to stay for so long. She talked to her children who were crying because they missed her and she wanted to go home but Barry was insistent that he had everything under control. Actually, he sounded angry and gave the excuse that it was costly and a waste of money to fly back and then fly off again to Keena.

Mandy reassessed the situation; Barry and money were not on the top of her priority list at the moment. The next day, she called her children again to find out how their disposition was. They were calm and happy so she asked them if she could stay a little longer. They agreed and Mandy relaxed.

When Mandy arrived at Keena airport, Barry came with the children to pick her. He had driven all the way with the children from Mutalin to Keena. His uncle offered to push the trolley but Mandy, who had recuperated and was strong enough, declined the offer.

In the car, Barry talked non-stop to his uncle. He had not said one word to Mandy. Mandy was sadly aware of this but continued to play and hug her children who were so excited to see their mother.

They arrived at his uncle's house and Mandy went upstairs to unpack. Barry had taken her bags into the room earlier and left to continue his chatter with his uncle.

They had an appointment to see the oncologist in the General Hospital the next day. Mandy got up early, got dressed and having lost much of her hair from the treatment, put on a wig. They drove to the General Hospital in silence. This was the first day in the days ahead that they drove to the General Hospital in silence.

It was a separate building from the hospital and it was well laid out. There was even a rock garden with a small fountain in one corner. It was air-conditioned and there was a TV and a water dispenser.

Mandy had brought her walkman and switched it on to occupy her thoughts. The lively music kept her spirits up. Music played a very important part in her recovery.

Soon, they called her name. She went in through sliding metal doors that looked like they belong to a lift. Once inside, a team of three was ready and waiting for her.

'Please take off your blouse and lie down here,' said the young lady gently.

Then the team went to work marking, measuring and adjusting her so the radiation rays would hit the target just right.

The staff at the radiotherapy department were well-trained and very friendly. Mandy was self-conscious at first but soon relaxed. Keena was the cancer centre of the region and Mandy was thankful she was not the first patient.

She would repeat the same routine daily except for public holidays and weekends. Soon, she got to know the names of the staff and was even able to joke and accept compliments from them.

At the waiting area, Mandy saw several patients with their caregivers or family with them. Mandy saw husbands sitting close to their wives, holding their hands and talking softly to them. She saw daughters accompanying their mothers, talking to them. She saw patients dressed in green hospital gowns, most were depressed, accompanied by their nurse while there were a few who were quite independent and walking by themselves. By now, Mandy could tell who the patient was and who was wearing a wig. She could tell who was depressed and who was handling it well.

One day, while walking to the counter to report herself, Mandy realized something. Some of the people sitting down were staring at her! Her daughter's words came back to her, "Mummy, you look so beautiful in a skirt!" or "Mummy, I like it when you put on red lipstick!"

Mandy supposed it was a little out of the ordinary that she came out of the radiotherapy room beaming widely and walking so energetically. Her sense of self began to rise again. She considered herself very lucky that she could still look good and it showed through her smile, her gait and her ease in bantering with the staff. Her walkman kept her sane and saved her at a time when she would have hit rock bottom.

It seemed strange that she did not dread going for radiotherapy sessions. Maybe this was because it was here that there was contact with the outside world. This was where people smiled and talked to her.

Mandy had little to look forward to each day other than her treatment. Her children provided the only relief for her. She was glad that with each session, she was drawing nearer to the end of her stay in Keena. How she wanted to go home!

Fill in the blanks below:

1) Mandy was hyper _____ when she told Barry about her desire to take a break.

2) Barry went to _____ after their conversation.

3) Mandy called her _____ before deciding to stay on longer in Sooba.

4) Mandy pushed the _____ by herself at the Keena airport.

5) The staff at the radiotherapy department was _____ and well-trained.

6) Her walkman kept her _____.

CHAPTER 12

Pushing on

F inally the day came for the last radiotherapy session. Mandy had gotten to know the staff well. Even those who hardly smiled could smile at her; it was such a positive feeling. The staff too knew it was her last session and there was a mixed feeling of sadness and finality in the air. It was as if one was preparing for a long journey, leaving friends, beginning a new life all over again.

Amy who was one of the staff at the radiotherapy unit was waiting for Mandy as she finished dressing.

'Remember not to use any soap on the affected area for at least a month. Just splash with water when you bathe. Don't worry about the darkened skin, it will return to normal in due time.'

Amy smiled warmly, patting Mandy on the shoulder at the same time.

'You can go to see the doctor now, he is waiting for you. Take care.'

Mandy shook hands and thanked her before proceeding to the doctor's office.

Mandy's father called her the night before.

'When will your next follow-up be?'

'I don't know, Dad. I will see the doctor tomorrow and he will tell me.'

'Ask if you can have the follow-up done in Sooba, all right?' Mandy's father encouraged.

'It will be better here for you as your mum and I are here.'

'You are right, Dad. Thanks for the suggestion. I will ask the doctor tomorrow.'

She flew to Sooba. Barry drove with the children to Mutalin. Before she left Keena and after she arrived in Sooba, she kept asking Barry if they were going to stop over in Sooba for a night before continuing the drive to Mutalin. Barry's response was vague.

On the day Barry and the children were leaving, Mandy kept trying to reach Barry by phone but she just could not get through. She tried in the morning, mid-morning and in the afternoon. Finally she got through.

'Hello? Barry? I've been trying to reach you all morning. Where are you?'

'Are you near Sooba now? Let's have lunch or tea together before you continue to Mutalin,' Mandy pleaded.

'We have passed Sooba an hour ago. We will be in Mutalin soon,' Barry said nonchalantly.

Mandy could not believe her ears. She was so disappointed. Barry had not realised she had been waiting for him and the kids in Sooba. Mandy's face would have lit up to see the children playing with their grandparents.

Mandy's father advised her to stay on for another two weeks before heading home. Mandy was just so relieved to be out of Keena. Mostly, she rested at home. She still did not watch television but she listened to the radio a lot. When she got tired of the songs on radio, she listened to the songs in her walkman.

Her parents were in the house most of the time, reading or watching television. Whenever her younger brother came back from work, he would look for her first. Her other sisters who were not staying in the same town would phone her and talk to her. Often her younger brother would ask her, "Mandy, do you want to go out tonight?"

"Where are you taking me?"

"Where would you like to go? Want to go for an ice-cream?"

Mandy beamed widely and Ted knew he had hit her weak point.

Mandy had a weakness for ice-cream especially when it is served in a cone. Even during her school days, she was always going to a grocery store near Endrica's house to buy some so they could enjoy it on their long walks in the evenings.

Mandy remembered her 2nd chemo when she was so miserable in the hospital. She was in the crowded ward. Barry came over and asked her if there was anything she wanted. It was a hot day and there was a fan at her bedside. Even then, she was very uncomfortable. She knew it seemed a little silly to ask for such a thing but she was so longing for one. "How about an ice-cream cone from the supermarket?"

Barry's forehead frowned and he narrowed his eyes at her. It was as if that was the most outrageous request she had ever made!

Mandy cringed and wished she had never opened her mouth. Days after she was out of the hospital, Barry brought his nephew to the supermarket and bought her the ice-cream . . . . he remembered!

Mandy felt warm under the wig and did not wear it at home. It had been almost two months after her last chemo and her hair was growing. There were no longer any bald patches; her new hair was flat like a baby's, very black and soft.

Mandy's mother and Ted remarked that she no longer needed to wear the wig; she had hair already but Mandy was sceptical and continued to wear her wig.

'Take off your wig and I'll take you shopping for trendier clothes to match your new hair style,' remarked Ted.

'I don't know . . . ,' Mandy hesitated.

Ted persisted; he wanted to see his sister happy especially after what she had been through. Finally Mandy agreed.

'You look marvellous!' Mandy's Dad commented when he saw Mandy without her wig and wearing her new clothes.

'You look like a teenager!' Mandy's Mum said. Ted said her wig was so fake-looking. Jim, her friend said she looked better with short hair rather than the mop she used to wear. Mandy laughed to hear such honest, no holds barred comments from the people close to her. Overall, the comments were very good about her new image.

Mandy went out to town confidently with her new look. Almost everywhere she went, she noticed out of the corner of her eye, men and women alike would stop and stare at her super-short hair.

Mandy's father chuckled and said, "You should put on your wig before flying home."

"Dad, I've gone around half of Sooba town already without my wig. Why should I put it on again?"

Mandy's father continued to smile widely, amused that his daughter could once again be so bubbly and confident. Mandy guessed that the people around her were trying to get used to her super-short hair; they had been so used to her flowing tresses in the past.

Questions:

1) Where did Mandy have all her follow-ups? Why?

2) Did Mandy leave Keena first?

3) Why couldn't Mandy see her children as they passed through Sooba?

4) Who encouraged Mandy to rest in Sooba before heading home?

5) Who always looked for Mandy when he got home?

6) What did Mandy have a weakness for?

CHAPTER 13

Rejuvenating

D uring her long stay in Keena, Mandy had the chance to meet other cancer patients especially in the hospital. They had a separate building for cancer patients, not that they were like leprosy-ridden people but rather because of the extensive care and treatment needed. It is a good thing as patients diagnosed with cancer are emotionally fragile and need understanding and support. It is also heartening to see other cancer patients and the way they deal positively with the disease.

On one of her visits to the doctor, Mandy was sitting behind a well-dressed woman. She too was wearing a wig, still very neat-looking. Her face was lightly made up and she was wearing high heeled sandals. The woman was sitting on the other side, two rows in front of Mandy. She took out her lipstick and touched up her lips. Out of her compact mirror, she saw Mandy looking at her. She turned and gave Mandy a smile that said, 'We are women, after all.'

Mandy smiled back in agreement. This was such a wonderful feeling. It was like telling each other that although they were suffering from cancer, such a death sentence in itself, they were still women and still humans. They still wanted to look good; they still wanted to feel good and one way women were so capable of doing this totally on their own was to groom themselves from head to toe.

You can definitely tell who was depressed and who was not from the outlook of a person. It shows in the way how she talks, walks and dresses. It also shows in the eyes as the eyes, they say, are the mirror to a person's soul.

You can also tell if the accompanying family member is supportive or not by their body language. Mandy saw husbands sitting close to their wives, holding their hands or putting an arm around their shoulders and talking softly.

Whenever Mandy felt lonely, the books and walkman distracted her and boosted her spirit. Even at nights, she would fall asleep listening to her walkman. She needed to hear positive things and have a happy environment. The music diverted her thoughts and calmed her.

There were a few questions which kept bugging Mandy—how do you handle life knowing you are going to die? How do you plan for death? How do you plan your life not knowing when you are going to die?

Some people tell Mandy that life is uncertain for everybody. Nobody knows when they are going to leave this world. That is true but the fact is that people who are healthy, people who do not have a life threatening disease, people like Mandy herself BEFORE the cancer diagnosis, do not think about death. Healthy people, unless they are very old, live each day thinking they will always see tomorrow.

Mandy asked a few cancer survivors those same questions. They all give the same answer. Don't think about death. Think positively. Do not worry too much about your problems. In short, live life to the fullest each and every day. Be happy every chance you get. This is the time to take care and nurture yourself. If it did not happen in the past, if you have always put others first, this is the time to put YOURSELF first. This is not selfish at all. It is only right. Only when you are happy can the people around you be happy. Do the things that bring you pleasure, rediscover your dreams!

Mandy read somewhere a line written by an Octogenarian. It was just a short simple sentence but it made a lasting impact. It read, "The things you regret in life are not the things you have done, but the things you HAVE NOT done."

Yes! Go climb a mountain. Go on an all girls' holiday. Learn a new skill. Go for a makeover! Buy that red dress! You will come back rejuvenated! Think of all the things you have always wanted to do but pushed aside due to this and that. Just thinking of the possibilities will make you smile. Do yourself a favour. If you can't make yourself happy, who can? It is your decision, your choice.

All too soon, it was time for Mandy to go home to Mutalin, where Barry and her children were waiting. As she stepped out of the car, her children came running out of the house, jumping up and down. They were so happy to see her.

"Yea . . . . Mummy is home! Mummy is home!"

They said over and over again. Mandy was happy to be home. She happily hugged all her children.

"Come on. Let's go in and see what toys Mama has bought for three of you."

The children happily skipped into the house with their mother.

It felt good to see her children but a little strange to be back in the house after such a long absence. Mandy had not gotten used to being out of the house without the children. The children were so excited and happy. They were smiling from ear to ear. They could not wait to see the toys bought by their mother.

In the following days, her children followed her around like a second shadow. Whenever Mandy went upstairs, they would follow. If she were to stay in the toilet a little longer, her daughters would be calling, "Mummy! Mummy! Where are you?"

If she went outside to the veranda, her Hung would be calling her. Mandy loved her children very much.

Mandy was happy to take care of the children now that she was strong again in mind and body. When she was undergoing chemo treatment, she was really weak but still she found the energy within herself to take care of the kids, especially when Barry or the maid was not around.

Mandy started going marketing with the maid in town. The vegetable vendors were asking her where she had been. They had not seen her for a while. Mandy good-humouredly said she went home for a holiday. She enjoyed marketing for her family, buying their favourite vegetable or food. She also enjoyed cooking for her children, tempting their appetites with a different dish each day. Making her family happy had always been satisfying for her.

True / False statements. Circle the correct answer.

1) They have a separate building for cancer patients. T/F

2) Mandy could fall asleep easily at night without any help. T/F

3) Healthy people live each day thinking they will see tomorrow. T/F

4) The kids were happy and excited to see their mother. T/F

5) Mandy refused to do any marketing for her family. T/F

6) Barry was pleased with Mandy's progress and had a lot to say. T/F

CHAPTER 14

The Phone call

M andy wanted to improve herself and expand her children's horizon so she decided to take up guitar lessons during the weekends. She would drive to Sooba and enrol in a music school there. At the same time, her kids will come with her and enjoy spending some quality time with their grandparents.

A friend once remarked to Mandy that if she does not challenge herself to learn, she would never grow. Perhaps that was what life was all about, challenging oneself so as to continue to have zest for living.

'Barry, I am planning to take up guitar lessons in Sooba during the weekends.

There was silence and a stony expression as usual. He did not even bother to put down the newspaper when he answered, 'That's too far away. Why can't you get the teacher to come here?'

Mandy sighed, 'Of course I will look into that possibility. You don't have to worry about that. Anyway, I think it will be good for the kids too. It will only be for the weekends.'

Barry kept silent and continued to read his newspaper. Mandy walked off.

'Round one', she thought.

The next day, Patricia called Mandy up for breakfast. She was thrilled that Mandy had decided to take up guitar lessons in Sooba.

'Good for you! You should not be stuck up in the house all day long. Even a healthy person would fall ill living like that.'

Mandy smiled.

Patricia had been her friend for many years now. She was not very pretty but she projected a very 'no nonsense' image. Mandy liked her out-spoken personality. She was not afraid to speak her mind especially when things were not to her liking.

She looked pleasant with her wavy shoulder length hair which she usually left untied. Mandy often remarked on Patricia's fair skin. She answered Mandy good naturedly that only a pure, unadulterated line of mainland Chinese could have this kind of effect.

Patricia runs her own business selling cosmetics. It was not easy at the beginning pushing people to buy her brand but she kept at it. She had to when she thought of her husband whose employment was so unreliable. She also has three school-going children who needed to be fed, clothed and educated. The cost of education was only going higher with each passing year.

That was five years ago. Now she has a shop in a busy part of town and three loyal employees. Her husband gave up working altogether and helped her out in the shop. It hurt Patricia to hear that the local community thinks she married a worthless husband who could not even support his wife. It hurt her even more to hear that her husband went on trips with other women.

Mandy called up the music school in Sooba and asked if they could send any guitar teacher out-station to teach. They said they could, provided that there was a minimum of 10 participants.

'Well, I tried,' thought Mandy. 'Where in the world am I going to find 10 people in this small town who are interested in music? I might as well save myself the trouble and drive over to Sooba.'

The kids were so happy when Mandy told them they were going on a trip to see their grandparents. The kids loved trips.

Before the planned trip to Sooba, Mandy told Barry.

'Why didn't you tell me earlier? I need time to plan my schedule!' He was clearly upset.

'I DID tell you! I also told you I will look into the possibility of getting the teacher here but since I can't, we'll enjoy the one hour ride. My parents are there and this is a wonderful opportunity for them to get to know our kids!' Mandy was fuming. She had spent a lot of time making the arrangements.

Barry's mind was racing.

'I will not be able to join you because I have an important business trip tomorrow. I am flying off to Kinol to clinch a deal.'

Mandy cancelled the trip, got into her car and started driving. She did not know where she was going. She only knew she had to get out of the house. She was so angry!

She did not come home until two hours later, her anger still there but a little subdued. She asked the kids if they had showered and eaten their dinner yet. They had. She went for a shower after ruffling the kids' hair.

Barry started packing the night before the weekend.

The company driver sent Barry to the airport the next morning. He left after kissing the kids.

Mandy took out the vegetables from the refrigerator. The broccoli would go well with some julienne carrot strips. She would braise some chicken with potato wedges. Her elder daughter would love the gravy. She would always spoon the gravy all over her rice. Her younger daughters could eat the potatoes as they liked everything else but rice.

The children were watching television in the living room. Mandy made a mental note to get them to do some homework in an hour's time. She took out the chicken thighs which were half defrosted and put them in a plastic basin. Next, she cut up the broccoli into florets and soaked them in another plastic basin. Since there were only 3 of them for lunch, she did not cook much. She stopped slicing the chicken meat off the bones and wondered if Barry was coming home for dinner. As usual, his replies were vague.

Well, if he did come back, then she would just heat up some canned food to supplement the existing dishes. She did not think anymore of it as she concentrated on cutting the veins out of the meat.

The phone rang that night when Mandy and her children were comfortably seated in front of the television. Her youngest rushed to pick it up.

'Mummy, I think it's for you. The man sounds funny.'

Mandy took the phone from her, curious as to who would call her at that time of the night.

'Is this Mrs. Barry Hawitt?' The voice was serious and Mandy felt tense all of a sudden.

'Yes.' Mandy answered nervously.

'I am Mr. Les Madin from the Kinol Airport. We have some bad news. The plane your husband was on has met with an accident . . . .'

Mr. Les Madin continued talking but Mandy had already dropped the hand set. She suddenly felt cold all over. She sank to the floor, a dazed expression on her face.

True /False statements. Circle the correct answer.

1) Barry liked the idea of Mandy and the kids going for guitar lessons. T/F

2) Patricia was timid. T/F

3) Patricia was selling kitchenware. T/F

4) The kids were happy to be going to Sooba to take up guitar lessons. T/F

5) Barry said he was going to Jakarta. T/F

6) Barry called home the night after he left. T/F

DICTIONARY PORTION

Adrenaline—a hormone that increases rates of heart beat, especially in stressful conditions

Agitated—Anxious/excited

Anxiety—overwhelming sense of apprehension and fear

Assault—an attempt to inflict offensive bodily harm

Authoritative—in a confident manner

Awe—respectful and scared

Bantering—speaking in a witty and teasing manner

Beaming—smiling with joy

Bedpan—a shallow container used by a bedridden person for urination or defecation

Biopsy—the examination of tissue taken from somebody in order to find out more about their disease

Bitterly—with great sadness

Braced—to be prepared for an attack

Braise—to cook slowly in fat and little liquid in a closed pot

Breakneck—very fast

Briefed—given detailed instructions

Broken—consumed by grief

Cajoled—try to persuade someone to do something by talking in a soft and gentle manner

Camouflage—disguise by covering or painting so as to blend in with their surroundings

Cascaded—fell in large quantities

Chuckled—laughed quietly

Civilians—people not in the army or the police force

Client—a person paying for the services of a professional person or organization

Cocked—tilted

Cold feet—become afraid or nervous

Compliments—admiring remarks

Concurred—agreed

Confessed—admitted

confidence—belief that one is capable

Consultation—professional advice

Conviction—quality of being sincere

Cool—not friendly

Crane—a machine for lifting and moving heavy things by using a swinging arm

Cringed—to shrink in fear

Dampen—to become depressed

Dazed—astonished or disbelief

Delirious—cannot think, disturbed

Demure—reserved and modest

Denial—in a state of refusal to believe that something is true

Diaper—a piece of soft cloth folded round a baby's bottom and between its legs

Dimly—not bright

Disposition—mood

Distressed—worried or troubled

Doe eyes—big and gentle eyes

Ecstatic—overwhelmingly happy

Enthusiasm—great enjoyment

Established—firm and not in danger of closing down at any time

Exasperated—irritated and annoyed

Exasperated—irritated greatly

Exemplary—excellent

Exhilarating—cheerful and exciting

Exquisitely—very

Fastidious—paying attention to accuracy and detail

Fault—mistake

Flagging—weak

Flare—a burst of flame or light shot from a gun

Flipped—turned over quickly

Florets—a cluster of flower buds

Footways—a small lane

Foregone conclusion—an easily predictable result

Frazzled—tired and stressed

Frown—expression showing disapproval, displeasure or concentration

Fuming—very angry

Gaiety—the state of being happy and cheerful

Gait—a manner of walking

Goggle—stare, openly admiring

Good-humouredly—cheerfully

Gratified—pleased

Grim—not in a happy or relaxed manner

Gushed—spoke quickly

Hearty—Displaying cheerful and friendly feelings

Heightened—peaked

Climbing the Mountain

Horizon—circumference of experience

Horn-rimmed spectacles—spectacles with frames made of a horn-like material

Housebound—having difficulty leaving the house

Household name—well-known name

Humid—a high level of water vapour in the atmosphere

Hyperventilating—to breathe rapidly and deeply, usually caused by stressful situations

Impending—scary and cannot be avoided

Impressed—gained the admiration of

Infantry—soldiers who fight on foot

Insistent—stubborn in spite of opposition or warning

Insolent—very rude

Jolting—to roughly, abruptly cause something

Keenly—extremely

Lacked—short of

Lacking—missing

Learn the ropes—get familiar with the routine

Leprosy—an infectious disease affecting the skin

Lively—energetic

Angela Aw

Marvelous—notably more beautiful

Metastasis—the spread of a disease from the initial site of disease to another part of the body

Milestone—a significant new development or stage

Misted—going to cry

Morbid—characterized by gloomy or unwholesome feelings

Nausea—an urge to vomit

Neglected—gave not enough care to something

Neutral territory—place that does not side or assist either side in a war

Nonchalantly—with unconcerned indifference

Nuisance—a thing that is annoying

Nurture—nourish

Octogenarian—a person whose age is in the eighties

On edge—scared

Ordeals—difficult experience

Outrageous—beyond what is right or decent

Paid off—a deserved reward

Panicked—felt uncontrollable fear

Persistent—happening frequently

Personnel—people working in a company

Plodded—walked heavily

Poised—ready and prepared

Preliminary—preparatory

prim—proper and stiff

Prominent—easily noticeable

Proposed—to make an offer of marriage

Pursed—puckered

Ragged—not even

Recognised—knew and remembered

Recuperated—to recover health

Regret—feel very sorry for

Reluctant—not willing and slow to act

Renovation—improving a building

Resolved—decided firmly

Reverberating—repeating over and over again

Route—road

Rubble—pieces of a destroyed building

Ruffling—to make into a confused mass

Sceptical—with doubts

Scrumptious—extremely good to eat

Seasoned—having much experience

Secure—safe

Self-conscious—uncomfortably conscious of oneself

Simultaneously—happening at the same time

Singlets—sleeveless garment

Soared—sudden increase to a high level

Soothe—to comfort

Soothing—comforting

Stammered—spoke in a nervous way

Stony—without expression

Stormed—moved in an angry manner

Subdued—lacking in intensity

Suckling—breastfeeding

Supreme—highest level

Surged—raced in big amounts

Sympathised—felt compassion for

Tedious—slow and difficult

Thatched—a roof covered with straw, reeds or similar material

Tote—a large two-handled open-topped bag, usually made of canvas

Transfixed—as if hypnotized

Tresses—long unbound hair of a woman

Trigger—a device that one presses in order to fire a gun

Triplets—three children born to the same mother at one time

Ultrasound—a non-invasive way used for the examination of bodily abnormalities

Unadulterated—pure

Unfocused—unable to concentrate on anything

Vague—not clear

Vein—blood vessel

Veranda—a roofed open gallery attached to the exterior of a building

Vivacious—beautiful and lively

Vividly—strong clear images in the mind

Void of expression—With no emotion

Volatile—likely to change rapidly, especially for the worse

Warmly—with affection

Washboard torso—the part of the body below the chest and above the hips which looks like a board with ridges on it.

Whining—distressed crying

Wincing—to hurt from pain

Worthless—of no use

Zest—keen feeling of enjoyment

Zombie—a human not capable of coherent thinking